Shells!

Shells!

Written and Illustrated by

Nancy Elizabeth Wallace

Marshall Cavendish Children

Special thanks to Heather Leigh Toothaker, Director of Education, Schooner, Inc., for reading the manuscript. Schooner, Inc. is a nonprofit organization dedicated to promoting environmental awareness and personal growth by providing educational experiences in marine science, sailing, and the history of Long Island Sound and its watershed. Hands-on instruction occurs at shore sites, in community centers, schools, and aboard the traditional gaff-rigged, red-sailed, ninety-one-foot schooner, *Quinnipiack*. For more information, visit:

www.schoonerinc.org

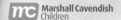

Text and illustrations copyright © 2007 by Nancy Elizabeth Wallace
All rights reserved

Marshall Cavendish Corporation
99 White Plains Road, Tarrytown, NY 10591
www.marshallcavendish.us

The text for this book is set in 16 pt Triplex Sans Bold.
The illustrations are rendered in cut paper.
Bookmark hand lettering by Ruth Estella Boehling.
Book design by Virginia Pope.

Printed in China
First edition

1 2 3 4 5 6

Library of Congress Cataloging-in-Publication Data
Wallace, Nancy Elizabeth.
Shells! shells! shells! / written and illustrated by Nancy Elizabeth Wallace.
p. cm.
Summary: When Buddy Bear and his mother go to the beach, she teaches him all about shells and mollusks.
Includes facts about shells.
ISBN 978-0-7614-5332-1
[1. Shells—Fiction. 2. Mollusks—Fiction. 3. Mothers—Fiction. 4. Bears—Fiction.] I. Title.
PZ7.W15875She 2006
[E]—dc22
2006012992

To my mom, Alexine, and my husband, Peter,
and to shell lovers everywhere!

—N.E.W.

Early one spring morning, Buddy and his mother went to the beach.

As they walked, the cold water tickled their toes. It was low tide.

There were lots of shells. Buddy picked some up and dropped them into his bucket.

As he did, he said, "She sells sea shells by the seashore."

He said it faster. "Shesellsseashellsbythe . . ." Suddenly Buddy stopped.

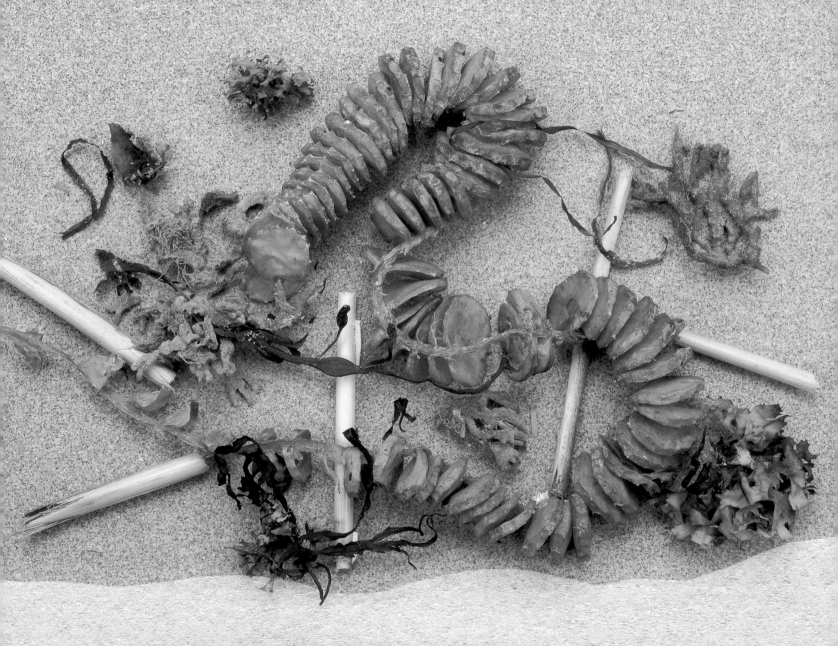

"Wow! Look at this, Mama!"

Buddy touched it. "It feels dry and crumbly."
He shook it. "It rattles."
"It's an egg case," said Mama.
"Open one of the pouches."
Buddy pinched off a pouch . . .

. . . and carefully broke it open.
He shook what was inside onto Mama's scarf.

"Wow! Teeny tiny shells! Shells! Shells!"
Then he asked, "What makes shells?"
Mama said, "Animals called *mollusks.*"

Buddy picked two shells out of his bucket. He looked at them. "I don't see any mollusks."

Mama said, "They were animals that once lived inside the shells. The hard shells protected their soft bodies."

"Is a shell a mollusk's house?"

"It's a mollusk's skeleton!" said Mama.
Buddy felt his bones. "Skeleton! My skeleton is on the inside!"
Mama said, "Some animal skeletons are on the inside, some are on the outside!"

"How do mollusks make shell skeletons?"

Mama explained, "Mollusks have a part of their bodies that is like skin. It's called the *mantle*.
The mantle makes shell-building liquid. Shells are made of layers and layers and layers of shell-building liquid that gets hard."

Buddy looked at another shell. "I see layers!"

Mama said, "Good looking! A mollusk makes the layers as it grows. The shell-building material comes from the mollusk's food and water."

"Food!" said Buddy. "I'm hungry! Let's eat."

Buddy and Mama had breakfast.
"Mama?"
"Yes, Buddy."

"What did the octopus have for breakfast?"
"What?"
"Toast with butter and *shelly*!"
Mama laughed.

After breakfast Buddy said, "I want to look for *more* shells."

"Okay!" said Mama.

They combed the beach.

Then they spread the shells they had collected on the blanket.

"Look!" said Buddy.

"What do you see?" asked Mama.

"Lots of different kinds of shells:

Scallop shells

Clam shells

Mussel shells

Oyster shells

Razor clam shells

Whelk shell

Slipper shells

Jingle shells!"

Moon snail shell

"What else do you see?" asked Mama.

"Lots of different shapes!
  Some are little, some are big,
    some are long and skinny,
      some are smooth, some are bumpy,
        some are shiny."

Buddy jumped up. "I'm going to get *MORE* shells!"

When he came back, Buddy spread six scallop shells on the blanket. He sat there for a minute thinking.

"These shells look the same, but different! Some are really dark. One has stripes. I see different colors! How does that happen?" Buddy asked.

"Some mollusks have a part of their bodies that makes colors. It's called the *pigment center*. The pigment center can add color to the liquid that makes the shell," said Mama.

"*PIG*-ment center! Oink! Oink Oink!" shouted Buddy. "I don't see any pigs!"

"Oink! Oink! Oink!" said Mama. "Me neither. What do you think pigment means?"

"Color!" said Buddy.

Buddy picked up a scallop shell and felt it. "These shells are the bumpiest."
Mama said, "Bumpy ribs help make shells strong."
"I have ribs!" said Buddy.

"And you have ears," said Mama. "Scallop shells have ears, too! The triangles at the bottom are called ears!"

"Ears!" said Buddy.

"I see something else," said Buddy. "I see where this shell grew a *lot*."

"Yes, Bud," said Mama. "When there's a lot of food and the temperature is warm, the mollusk and its shell will grow more."

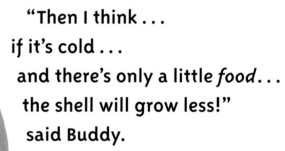

"Then I think . . . if it's cold . . . and there's only a little *food* . . . the shell will grow less!" said Buddy.

"I think you are very smart," said Mama.

"Did I say FOOD?" asked Buddy. "'Cause I'm hungry! Let's eat!"

Buddy and Mama had a snack.

"Mama, do you know which shells are really strong?"
"Which?"
"Mussel shells!"
Mama chuckled.

After their snack, Buddy piled up jingle shells.
Then he sorted them. "Orange jingle shells.
Black jingle shells. Yellow jingle shells. The yellow ones look like money! Like gold!"
Mama said, "When I was your age, we called yellow jingle shells *pirate's gold*."

Then Buddy built a sand castle.
"Mama, what is sand?"
She explained, "Sand is tiny pieces of rock and shell."

Buddy poured water into the castle's moat.

"I'm looking for a door for my castle. But look at this clam shell I found. It has a big crack."

Mama said, "That crack *is* very big. If it had been a small crack, the mollusk could have patched it with the same liquid that made its shell!"

"Really? WOW!" said Buddy.

"Hmmmm," said Mama. "You still need a door for your castle. I just remembered I found . . ." Mama reached into the purple pail. "An *operculum*."

"O—PER—CUE—LUM?" said Buddy. "What's that?"

"Look at this whelk shell," said Mama. "Look at the opening. An operculum is part of a whelk mollusk. When the mollusk pulls itself inside its shell, the operculum covers the opening like a door. "

"DOOR!" said Buddy. "Cool!"

"Nice castle, Bud!" said Mama.

"There's something else I want to find," said Buddy. He set off again.

When he returned, he showed Mama. "Look what I found. Two shells together. Do they have a special name?"

"Hinged shells are *bivalves*," said Mama.

"Hinges! So the clam can open and close, open and close, open and close!" said Buddy.

"Yes! And *bi* means two. Something you ride has *bi* in the word."

"My *bi*cycle!" said Buddy. "It has two wheels!"

Mama showed Buddy a whelk shell and a moon snail shell.
"Single shells are called *univalves*," she said.

She pulled more spiral shells out of the purple pail and put them on the blanket.

Buddy looked. "I see how these shells grew!"

"Mollusks that live inside univalves have a fancy name," said Mama. "*Gastropods*."

"What? Gas! Do they have gas?" He giggled.

"Noooo," said Mama. "But you'll like this. *Gastropod* means . . . stomach foot!"

"Stomach foot? Stomach!" Buddy rubbed his stomach. "I'm hungry. Let's eat!"

He and Mama had lunch.

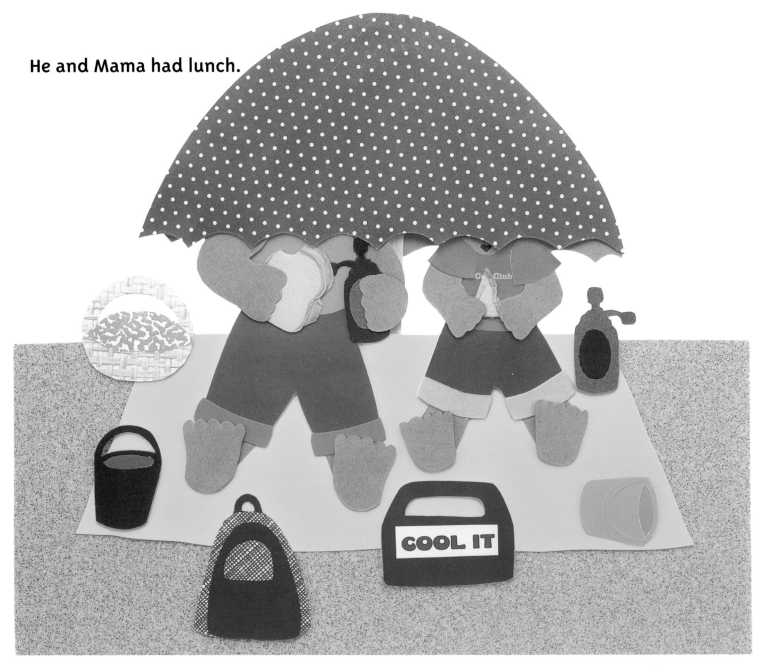

Buddy asked, "What song do shells sing in the winter when it's snowing?"
"What, Bud?"
"Jingle Shells! Jingle Shells! Jingle all the way."
Mama joined in.

"It's almost time to go, Bud," said Mama. "You can choose a few shells to take home."

Buddy put a spiral shell up to his ear.
"It sounds like the ocean!"
"Isn't that awesome?" said Mama.

Buddy asked, "Do all shells come from the ocean?"
Mama answered, "Most of the mollusks that make shells live in water—in oceans, in rivers, in ponds—where they can keep their bodies wet. Some mollusks live on land, in the forest. Some even live in the desert!"

"Wow!" said Buddy.

Mama looked at her watch. "Okay, my young *conchologist* . . ."

Cub Club

"What's that?"
"Someone, like you, who collects shells and looks at shells and learns all about shells."

"Kon-ko-lol—looooh-gist!" said Buddy.
Mama said, "Time to go home, conchologist."

Buddy picked eight shells and put them in his bucket.

COOL IT

Cub Club

"Mama?"

"Yes, Bud?"

"What did the tide say to the beach?"

"What, Bud?"

"I shell return!"

Did You Know?

Hermit crabs borrow empty shells to live in. As a crab grows bigger, it moves to bigger, empty shells.

The edges of univalves are called lips.

Giant clam shells can grow so big that they can be used as a bathtub! They can be found in the warm water of the South Pacific and the Indian Ocean. They sometimes grow as long as four feet, weigh up to 400 pounds, and live to be 100 years old.

Shells of land snails are thinner and lighter to carry.

Some Native American tribes carved the purple part of quahog shells into tiny beads called *wampum*. They made bead necklaces and bracelets, sewed them onto clothes, and wove shell beads into belts.

Spiral shells can be made into musical instruments.

If you see a tiny, round hole in a shell, it may have been made by a moon snail or an oyster drill. These are mollusks that eat other mollusks. They drill the holes with their long, rough tongues. Then they suck the other mollusks out and eat them.

Shells have been used as money and as dishes for food.

Orange jingle shells are sometimes called *Mermaid's Fingernails*. Black jingle shells are sometimes called *Grandpa's Toenails*.

Make an "I SHELL RETURN" bookmark

You will need:

Colored paper   Recycled paper
Scissors   A glue stick
A pencil   A pen

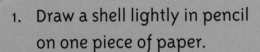

1. Draw a shell lightly in pencil on one piece of paper.

2. Cut out your shell. You can cut out and glue ribs or a swirl or an operculum onto your shell if you want to add more detail.

3. Cut out a long strip from another piece of paper, straight or wavy.

4. Glue the paper shell to the paper strip.

5. If you made a plain paper strip, you can write I SHELL RETURN on it in ink.

6. Read a book! Use your bookmark!

A shell bookmark makes a nice gift, too.

5 ½"

1 ½"

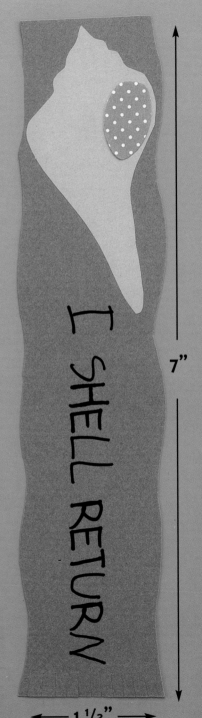

I SHELL RETURN

7"

1 ½"

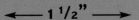

Warm Water Shells